TEDD ARNOLD

HUGGLY'S CHRISTMAS

SCHOLASTIC INC.

Cartwheel B·O·O·K·S ®

New York   Toronto   London   Auckland   Sydney
Mexico City   New Delhi   Hong Kong

For Christopher, Matthew, Eric, and Haley
— T. A.

Copyright © 2001 by Tedd Arnold.
All rights reserved. Published by Scholastic Inc.
HUGGLY and THE MONSTER UNDER THE BED are trademarks and/or registered trademarks of Tedd Arnold.
SCHOLASTIC, CARTWHEEL BOOKS, and associated logos are trademarks and/or registered trademarks of Scholastic Inc.

Library of Congress Cataloging-in-Publication Data available

ISBN: 0-439-13500-1

12 11 10 9 8 7 6 5 4 3   01 02 03 04 05 06

Printed in the U.S.A.
First printing, November 2001

Huggly climbed out from under the people child's bed and began to explore. He noticed a dark place in the bedroom. "I've never been here before," he whispered to himself. "Good thing I brought my star crystal to help me see." He played with some of the interesting people stuff.

Suddenly Huggly heard footsteps. "Yikes!" he said. "Someone is coming. I'd better go before I get caught!" He dived back under the bed.

"I'll just go play with Booter and Grubble," Huggly said as he headed for the Secret Slime Pit.

The people child came into the bedroom and dressed for bed. When he went to his closet he saw an unusual light. "Mom," he called. "Look what I found!"

"Not now, Wallace," said his mom. "It's time for bed. Remember, tomorrow is Christmas."

"Ple-e-e-ease," Wallace begged. "Can I just do one thing with this cool rock I found?"

"Okay," she said. "Then straight to bed."

Some time later, Huggly, Booter, and Grubble sat around their slime pit trying to decide what to play. After much discussion, Grubble said, "Why don't we go explore dark tunnels?"

"Yeah!" said Huggly. "Maybe we can find a bigger slime pit."

"Okay!" Booter agreed. "But some tunnels are really dark. Let's take our star crystal. Where is it?"

"Oops," said Huggly. "I just had it. I must have left it in the people child's room."

"No problem," said Grubble. "Let's go get the crystal, then we can go exploring."

The people child was
asleep and the house
was quiet when Huggly,
Booter, and Grubble
climbed out from under
the bed.

"It's gone!" Huggly gasped, looking inside the dark closet.
"Maybe he took it," said Grubble, pointing to the sleeping child.
"It was our best and only star crystal," Huggly whimpered.
"I really want it back."

Booter patted Huggly's shoulder. "Don't worry. We'll find it. It's probably in the house somewhere."

They tiptoed out of the bedroom and peeked through each and every doorway.

"It must be down there," whispered Huggly.

Together they climbed down the stairs. Huggly was curious about the plants growing on the railing.

"Look down here," said Grubble. "The people child didn't put all of his toys away."

"And look at this," said Booter. "He didn't finish his dinner."

"And he didn't even put all of his clothes away," said Huggly. "He must be a naughty people child."

Then they saw something that stopped them in their tracks. A tree full of lights was growing in the house! They couldn't believe their eyes.

"It's beau-u-u-tiful," Huggly whispered. Then he said, "Look! That's our crystal on top!"

Huggly stepped up onto a stuffed chair, but the star crystal was still high above him. "I can't reach it!" he cried.

"I have an idea," said Grubble.

Grubble hopped onto Booter's back. "Now climb on top of us," she said. Huggly began to climb onto his friends, but he tangled his toes in Grubble's hair and tumbled to the floor.

"I know what we can do," said Booter. "We'll fling you up." Booter and Grubble joined hands. Huggly stepped into their arms, and they launched him in the air.

"A-a-a-argh!" Huggly screamed. He crashed into the tree halfway up. But he still could not reach the crystal. "I'll just try to climb the rest of the way," he said.

When Huggly reached the top, the tree began to bend and sway. Just as it started to fall, Huggly grabbed the star crystal and jumped. Booter and Grubble ran to catch him but the tree caught *them* instead.

"We just made a lot of noise," said Grubble. "Let's get out of here!"

"Wait! We have to fix this tree first," said Huggly. "It was so-o-o beautiful."

"You're right," said Booter. "Monsters must always leave people stuff the way they found it. But let's hurry."

They did their best
to put the tree back
together the way it was
when they first saw it.

"Now can we go?" pleaded Grubble. "I think I hear someone coming."

"Wait!" said Huggly. "It wasn't like this." He looked up at the tree then down at the star crystal in his hand. "*This* is what made it beautiful. If it's okay with you two, I'm going to put it back. It will be like a present from us to the people child."

"Okay," said Booter.

"Fine! Whatever!" said Grubble. "Just HURRY!!!"

Once the star crystal was back on top of the tree, the three friends hurried away. But Huggly stopped to take one last look at the tree filled with lights. "It's so-o-o beautiful," he said.

Suddenly he heard a footstep. "Yes, it *is* beautiful," said a people voice.

Huggly froze with fear. A big, red people person was right beside him! He had no idea where the person had come from. He just knew getting caught by a people person was the worst thing that could happen to a monster. Huggly gulped and his knees trembled.

But the big, red person just smiled and winked his eye. Then he reached down and held out a small, bright box.

Huggly didn't know what to do. He grabbed the box from the people person, whirled around, and ran away as fast as his little legs could carry him. Climbing the stairs, Huggly could hear the sound of laughing: "Ho, ho, ho."

Back under the bed, Huggly found Booter and
Grubble waiting. He sat down on a rock to catch
his breath.

"Well," he said, "we can always find another
star crystal."

"How?" said Grubble. "They only grow at the ends of long dark tunnels."

"What's that?" asked Booter, pointing to the little box.

"I don't know." said Huggly. "A big, red people person gave it to me." He unwrapped the box.

Huggly pulled out a small object with a red button on its side. He pushed the button and a light came on.

"Wow! It's some kind of light stick," Huggly exclaimed. "Now we can explore those long dark tunnels. Let's go!"

And away they went.